Rockets

MY FUNNY FAMILY

Granny's Jungle Garden

Colin W

A & C Black • London

Rockets

MY FUNNY FAMILY - Colin West

Uncle-and-Auntie Pat
Granny's Jungle Garden
Jenny the Joker
Grandad's Boneshaker Bicycle

Reprinted 2005
First paperback edition 1999
First published 1999 in hardback by
A & C Black (Publishers) Ltd
37 Soho Square, London W1D 3QZ

www.acblack.com

ISBN 0-7136-4981-X

A CIP catalogue record for this book is available
from the British Library.

A & C Black uses paper produced with elemental
chlorine-free pulp, harvested from managed sustainable forests.

Printed and bound by G. Z. Printek, Bilbao, Spain.

Chapter One

This is a story about my granny.
I'm not sure how old she is.
When I ask her, all she says is,
'I'm older than yesterday, but
younger than tomorrow.'

I often go round to visit Granny.
She lives in a semi-detached house
not far from us.

Her house is like all the others in
the avenue...

Granny's
house

...but Granny's garden is very different to the other gardens. Over the years it's become more and more overgrown.

Next door to Granny lives Mr Smart.
He keeps his garden *very* tidy.

His flowers all stand to attention in neat rows...

...and his lawn is as smooth as a snooker table.

He clips his front hedge every
Tuesday...

...and he measures the grass every
Friday to see if it needs cutting.

Every year Mr Smart enters the
'Best kept Garden in Giggleswade'
Competition.

And for three years in a row, he's won
the Silver Watering Can Award.

Like Mr Smart, Granny spends a lot of time in the garden. But unlike Mr Smart, she doesn't spend much time actually gardening.

Granny prefers to sit quietly and
listen to the insects buzzing and the
birds singing.

Mr Smart is always dropping hints...

...and pointing out adverts in the
local paper.

But Granny doesn't take too much notice.

All the same, I could see that she was getting a bit worried by all his hints. So at the beginning of the summer holidays, I offered to lend a hand.

Chapter Two

Together, Granny and I got to work
on the garden. We chopped down
the nettles.

We cut back the brambles.

We dug up the weeds.

We mowed the lawn
and we rolled it flat.

We worked long and hard every day
for a fortnight.

At last Granny's garden looked almost as neat as Mr Smart's. We sat in deckchairs and looked around us.

'It certainly looks tidy,' said Granny.

'It certainly does,' I agreed.

And it certainly did.

Even Mr Smart was impressed.

But Granny noticed there weren't as many little visitors to her garden.

Chapter Three

The weeks went by, and with a little help, Granny's garden began to look more like it used to.

When Mr Smart saw how overgrown it was getting, he wasn't at all pleased.

He suggested a few things.

But this time, Granny didn't take any notice of him. She sat back and watched the grass grow.

She *liked*
the daisies...

...she *loved* the
buttercups...

...and she *adored*
the dandelions that
grew on her lawn.

As the nettles returned, so did the
beetles and the butterflies.

And as the brambles returned, so did the
birds and the bees.

We wanted to encourage even more wildlife, so we put up a bird table...

...then we dug a hole...

...and lined it with plastic to make a pond.

Soon we were watching birds feeding...

...and frogs and newts playing in the pond.

Not everyone was pleased, though.
Mr Smart for instance.

But Granny was happier than ever.
She loved spotting grasshoppers and
ladybirds.

Granny even made friends with a hedgehog who came to visit her every night. Her new improved jungle garden was her pride and joy.

Chapter Four

One afternoon, Granny and I were
putting scraps out for the birds
when I heard voices coming from
Mr Smart's garden.

Suddenly a stranger popped his head over the fence.

'Wildlife Sanctuary?' said Granny.

The stranger said his name was Duncan
Bennett.

Just then Mr Smart appeared at the
fence. He didn't look very happy.

Duncan Bennett went on:

Mr Smart began to fume quietly.

'May I come round?' asked Duncan.
'Please do!' said Granny.

Duncan explained about the competition.

Granny and I showed Duncan round.

As Duncan explored the jungle garden, he got more and more excited.

He made lots of notes, and then at last he asked:

Granny was almost lost for words, but at last managed to mutter 'yes'.

Chapter Five

A week later, Granny received the Silver Watering Can Award from Duncan Bennett. Everyone was overjoyed.

Everyone, that is, except Mr Smart.
He didn't agree with the result.

But there was nothing he could do
about it.

News soon spread about Granny's garden. Before long she was giving guided tours to complete strangers.

Other people in the avenue now appreciate Granny's garden too.

But most importantly, the birds, bees and butterflies all agree Granny's Jungle-Garden-Wildlife-Sanctuary is the best thing in all of Giggleswade.

THE END